STRENGTH FROM THE PSALMS

Verses to Comfort, Uplift, & Challenge

*compiled by Fritz Newenhuyse and
Elizabeth Cody Newenhuyse*

Harold Shaw Publishers
Wheaton, Illinois

Copyright © 1993 by Harold Shaw Publishers

Compiled by Fritz Newenhuyse and Elizabeth Cody Newenhuyse

ISBN 0-87788-799-3

Cover photo © 1993 by Robert Flesher

99 98 97 96 95 94

10 9 8 7 6 5 4 3 2

O God our Savior,
the hope of all the ends of the earth
and of the farthest seas . . .
You call forth songs of joy.

Psalm 65:5, 8, NIV

Contents

Contents

INTRODUCTION

The Psalms have comforted, uplifted, and challenged believers for thousands of years. Jesus himself drew frequently on their wisdom. So, too, should we.

These ancient songs tell of God's majesty—and his nearness. They instruct and they inspire. And, though ancient, their words are timeless. This book offers a selection of the Psalms' God-breathed wisdom and promises.

THE WONDER OF
HIS WORKS

Love all God's creation, the whole and
every grain of sand in it. Love every
leaf, every ray of God's light.
Fyodor Dostoevsky
The Brothers Karamazov

When I consider your heavens, the work of your fingers, the moon and the stars, which you have set in place, what is man that you are mindful of him, the son of man that you care for him? You made him a little lower than the heavenly beings and crowned him with glory and honor.

8:3-5, NIV

The earth is the LORD's and the fulness thereof, the world and those who dwell therein; for he has founded it upon the seas, and established it upon the rivers.

24:1-2, RSV

You visit the earth and water it, You greatly enrich it; the river of God is full of water; You provide their grain, for so You have prepared it. You water its ridges abundantly, You settle its furrows; You make it soft with show-

ers, You bless its growth. You crown
the year with Your goodness, and Your
paths drip with abundance. They drop
on the pastures of the wilderness, and
the little hills rejoice on every side.
The pastures are clothed with flocks;
the valleys also are covered with grain;
they shout for joy, they also sing.
65:9-13, NKJV

The day is yours, and yours also the
night; you established the sun and
moon. It was you who set all the
boundaries of the earth; you made
both summer and winter.
74:16-17, NIV

O Lord, what a variety you have made!
And in wisdom you have made them
all! The earth is full of your riches.
    There before me lies the mighty
ocean, teeming with life of every kind,
both great and small. And look! See

the ships! And over there, the whale you made to play in the sea. Every one of these depends on you to give them daily food. You supply it, and they gather it. You open wide your hand to feed them, and they are satisfied with all your bountiful provision.

But if you turn away from them, then all is lost. And when you gather up their breath, they die and turn again to dust.

Then you send your Spirit, and new life is born to replenish all the living of the earth. Praise God forever! How he must rejoice in all his work! The earth trembles at his glance; the mountains burst into flame at his touch.

I will sing to the Lord as long as I live. I will praise God to my last breath! 104:24-33, *TLB*

For you created my inmost being; you knit me together in my mother's womb.

I praise you because I am fearfully and wonderfully made; your works are wonderful, I know that full well. My frame was not hidden from you when I was made in the secret place. When I was woven together in the depths of the earth, your eyes saw my unformed body. All the days ordained for me were written in your book before one of them came to be.

139:13-16, NIV

OUR REFUGE AND STRENGTH

God is stronger than fire and destruction, and even in the valleys of deepest darkness, rod and staff are put into our hands and bridges are thrown across the abyss.

Helmut Thielicke

He lies in wait like a lion in cover; he lies in wait to catch the helpless; he catches the helpless and drags them off in his net. His victims are crushed, they collapse; they fall under his strength.
10:9-10, NIV

I will love You, O LORD, my strength. The LORD is my rock and my fortress and my deliverer; my God, my strength, in whom I will trust; my shield and the horn of my salvation, my stronghold. I will call upon the LORD, who is worthy to be praised; so shall I be saved from my enemies.
18:1-3, NKJV

You are my hiding place; you will protect me from trouble and surround me with songs of deliverance.
32:7, NIV

God is our refuge and strength, a very present help in trouble. Therefore we will not fear though the earth should change, though the mountains shake in the heart of the sea; though its waters roar and foam, though the mountains tremble with its tumult.

There is a river whose streams make glad the city of God, the holy habitation of the Most High. God is in the midst of her, she shall not be moved; God will help her right early. The nations rage, the kingdoms totter; he utters his voice, the earth melts. The LORD of hosts is with us; the God of Jacob is our refuge.
46:1-7, RSV

I am under vows to you, O God; I will present my thank offerings to you. For you have delivered me from death and my feet from stumbling,

that I may walk before God in the light of life.
56:12-13, NIV

You have purified us with fire, O Lord, like silver in a crucible. You captured us in your net and laid great burdens on our backs. You sent troops to ride across our broken bodies. We went through fire and flood. But in the end, you brought us into wealth and great abundance.
66:10-12, TLB

He who dwells in the shelter of the Most High, who abides in the shadow of the Almighty, will say to the LORD, "My refuge and my fortress; my God, in whom I trust." For he will deliver you from the snare of the fowler and from the deadly pestilence; he will cover you with his pinions, and under his wings you will find refuge; his faithfulness is a shield and buckler. You will not fear the terror of the night, nor the arrow that flies by day, nor the pestilence that stalks in darkness, nor the destruction that wastes at noonday.

91:1-6, RSV

GOD'S POWER AND MAJESTY

The universe is centered on neither the earth nor the sun. It is centered on God.

Alfred Noyes

The heavens are telling the glory of God; they are a marvelous display of his craftsmanship. Day and night they keep on telling about God. Without a sound or word, silent in the skies, their message reaches out to all the world. The sun lives in the heavens where God placed it and moves out across the skies as radiant as a bridegroom going to his wedding, or as joyous as an athlete looking forward to a race! The sun crosses the heavens from end to end, and nothing can hide from its heat.

19:1-6, TLB

The voice of the LORD is over the waters; the God of glory thunders, the LORD thunders over the mighty waters. The voice of the LORD is powerful; the voice of the LORD is majestic.

29:3-4, NIV

Let all the earth fear the LORD; Let all the inhabitants of the world stand in awe of Him. For He spoke, and it was done; He commanded, and it stood fast. The LORD brings the counsel of the nations to nothing; He makes the plans of the peoples of no effect, the counsel of the LORD stands forever, the plans of His heart to all generations.
33:8-11, NKJV

Many, O LORD my God, are the wonders you have done. The things you planned for us no one can recount to you; were I to speak and tell of them, they would be too many to declare. Sacrifice and offering you did not desire, but my ears you have pierced; burnt offerings and sin offerings you did not require. Then I said, "Here I am, I have come—it is written about me in the scroll."
40:5-7, NIV

. . . O God our Savior, the hope of all the ends of the earth and of the farthest seas, who formed the mountains by your power, having armed yourself with strength, who stilled the roaring of the seas, the roaring of their waves, and the turmoil of the nations. Those living far away fear your wonders; where morning dawns and evening fades you call forth songs of joy. *65:5-8, NIV*

Sing to God, you kingdoms of the earth; Oh, sing praises to the Lord, to Him who rides on the heaven of heavens, which were of old! Indeed, He sends out His voice, a mighty voice. Ascribe strength to God; His excellence is over Israel, and His strength is in the clouds. O God, You are more awesome than Your holy places. The God of Israel is He who

gives strength and power to His people. Blessed be God!
68:32-35, NKJV

I will call to mind the deeds of the LORD; yea, I will remember thy wonders of old. I will meditate on all thy work, and muse on thy mighty deeds. Thy way, O God, is holy. What god is great like our God? Thou art the God who workest wonders, who hast manifested thy might among the peoples. Thou didst with thy arm redeem thy people, the sons of Jacob and Joseph.

When the waters saw thee, O God, when the waters saw thee, they were afraid, yea, the deep trembled. The clouds poured out water; the skies gave forth thunder; thy arrows flashed on every side. The crash of thy thunder was in the whirlwind; thy lightnings lighted up the world; the earth trembled and shook. Thy way was through the sea, thy path through the great waters; yet thy footprints were unseen. Thou didst lead thy people like a flock by the hand of Moses and Aaron.

77:11-20, RSV

IN TIMES OF STRUGGLE

Afflictions are but the shadow of
God's wings.
George Macdonald

He says to himself, "God has forgotten; he covers his face and never sees." . . . But you, O God, do see trouble and grief; you consider it to take it in hand. The victim commits himself to you; you are the helper of the fatherless.
10:11, 14, NIV

Sing praise to the LORD, you saints of His, and give thanks at the remembrance of His holy name. For His anger is but for a moment, His favor is for life; weeping may endure for a night, but joy comes in the morning.
30:4-5, NKJV

Lord, all my longing is known to thee, my sighing is not hidden from thee. . . . But for thee, O LORD, do I wait; it is thou, O LORD my God, who wilt answer.
38:9, 15, RSV

When I am afraid, I will trust in you. In God, whose word I praise, in God I trust; I will not be afraid. What can mortal man do to me?
56:3-4, NIV

You are forgiving and good, O Lord, abounding in love to all who call to you. Hear my prayer, O LORD; listen to my cry for mercy. In the day of my trouble I will call to you, for you will answer me.
86:5-7, NIV

I love the Lord because he hears my prayers and answers them. Because he bends down and listens, I will pray as long as I breathe!

Death stared me in the face—I was frightened and sad. Then I cried, "Lord, save me!" How kind he is! How good he is! So merciful, this God of ours!

The Lord protects the simple and the childlike; I was facing death, and then he saved me. Now I can relax. For the Lord has done this wonderful miracle for me. He has saved me from death, my eyes from tears, my feet from stumbling. I shall live! Yes, in his presence—here on earth!
116:1-9, *TLB*

Those who sow in tears shall reap in joy. He who continually goes forth weeping, bearing seed for sowing, shall doubtless come again with rejoicing, bringing his sheaves with him.
126:5-6, *NKJV*

CARE FOR THE NEEDY

Man may dismiss compassion from
his heart, but God will never.
William Cowper

Lord, you know the hopes of humble people. Surely you will hear their cries and comfort their hearts by helping them. You will be with the orphans and all who are oppressed, so that mere earthly man will terrify them no longer.

10:17-18, TLB

"Because of the oppression of the weak and the groaning of the needy, I will now arise," says the Lord. "I will protect them from those who malign them."

12:5, NIV

But the meek shall inherit the earth, and shall delight themselves in the abundance of peace.

37:11, NKJV

A father to the fatherless, a defender of widows, is God in his holy dwell-

ing. God sets the lonely in families, he leads forth the prisoners with singing; but the rebellious live in a sun-scorched land.
68:5-6, NIV

He will respond to the prayer of the destitute; he will not despise their plea.
102:17, NIV

Some wandered in desert wastes, finding no way to a city to dwell in; hungry and thirsty, their soul fainted within them. Then they cried to the LORD in their trouble, and he delivered them from their distress; he led them by a straight way, till they reached a city to dwell in. Let them thank the LORD for his steadfast love, for his wonderful works to the sons of men! For he satisfies him who is thirsty, and the hungry he fills with good things.
107:4-9, RSV

Who is like the LORD our God, who dwells on high, who humbles Himself to behold the things that are in the heavens and in the earth? He raises the poor out of the dust, and lifts the needy out of the ash heap, that He may seat him with princes—with the princes of His people. He grants the barren woman a home, like a joyful mother of children. Praise the LORD!

113:5-9, NKJV

GOD'S PRESENCE

You are in the Beloved—his very own, his member. . . . You are never, not for one second, alone; then no reason for loneliness or depression.

Norman F. Douty

The boastful may not stand before thy eyes; thou hatest all evildoers.
5:5, RSV

The LORD is my shepherd; I shall not want. He makes me to lie down in green pastures; He leads me beside the still waters. He restores my soul; He leads me in the paths of righteousness for His name's sake. Yea, though I walk through the valley of the shadow of death, I will fear no evil; For You are with me; Your rod and Your staff, they comfort me.
23:1-4, NKJV

Blessed is he who has regard for the weak; the LORD delivers him in times of trouble. The LORD will protect him and preserve his life; he will bless him in the land and not surrender him to the desire of his foes.
41:1-2, NIV

Give your burdens to the Lord. He will carry them. He will not permit the godly to slip or fall.
55:22, *TLB*

I will come and proclaim your mighty acts, O Sovereign LORD; I will proclaim your righteousness, yours alone. Since my youth, O God, you have taught me, and to this day I declare your marvelous deeds. Even when I am old and gray, do not forsake me, O God, till I declare your power to the next generation, your might to all who are to come. Your righteousness reaches to the skies, O God, you who have done great things. Who, O God, is like you? Though you have made me see troubles, many and bitter, you will restore my life again; from the depths of the earth you will again bring me up. You will

increase my honor and comfort me
once again.
71:16-21, NIV

I bless the holy name of God with all
my heart. Yes, I will bless the Lord and
not forget the glorious things he does
for me.

He forgives all my sins. He heals
me. He ransoms me from hell. He sur-
rounds me with loving-kindness and
tender mercies. He fills my life with
good things! My youth is renewed
like the eagle's! He gives justice to all
who are treated unfairly. He revealed
his will and nature to Moses and the
people of Israel.

He is merciful and tender toward
those who don't deserve it; he is slow
to get angry and full of kindness and
love. He never bears a grudge, nor
remains angry forever. He has not pun-

ished us as we deserve for all our sins,
for his mercy toward those who fear
and honor him is as great as the height
of the heavens above the earth.
103:1-11, TLB

The LORD is with me; I will not be
afraid. What can man do to me?
118:6, NIV

I will lift up my eyes to the hills—from
whence comes my help? My help
comes from the LORD, who made
heaven and earth. He will not allow
your foot to be moved; He who keeps
you will not slumber. Behold, He who
keeps Israel shall neither slumber nor
sleep.
121:1-4, NKJV

I do not concern myself with great
matters or things too wonderful for

me. But I have stilled and quieted my
soul; like a weaned child with its
mother, like a weaned child is my soul
within me.

131:1-2, NIV

GOD'S FAITHFULNESS

God soon turns from his wrath, but he
never turns from his love.
Charles H. Spurgeon

The Lord himself is my inheritance, my prize. He is my food and drink, my highest joy! He guards all that is mine. He sees that I am given pleasant brooks and meadows as my share! What a wonderful inheritance! I will bless the Lord who counsels me; he gives me wisdom in the night. He tells me what to do.

I am always thinking of the Lord; and because he is so near, I never need to stumble or to fall.

Heart, body, and soul are filled with joy. For you will not leave me among the dead; you will not allow your beloved one to rot in the grave. You have let me experience the joys of life and the exquisite pleasures of your own eternal presence.

16:5-11, TLB

To the faithful you show yourself faithful, to the blameless you show

yourself blameless, to the pure you
show yourself pure, but to the
crooked you show yourself shrewd.
You save the humble but bring low
those whose eyes are haughty.
18:25-27, NIV

Though my father and mother forsake
me, the LORD will receive me.
27:10, NIV

O taste and see that the LORD is good!
34:8, RSV

Trust in the LORD, and do good; dwell
in the land, and feed on His faithfulness. Delight yourself also in the LORD,
and He shall give you the desires of
your heart. Commit your way to the
LORD, trust also in Him, and He shall
bring it to pass.
37:3-5, NKJV

I cry out to God Most High, to God, who fulfills his purpose for me. He sends from heaven and saves me, rebuking those who hotly pursue me; God sends his love and his faithfulness.

57:2-3, NIV

Lord, through all the generations you have been our home! Before the mountains were created, before the earth was formed, you are God without beginning or end.

90:1-2, TLB

For the LORD is good; His mercy is everlasting, and his truth endures to all generations.

100:5, NKJV

Though I walk in the midst of trouble, thou dost preserve my life; thou dost stretch out thy hand against the wrath

of my enemies, and thy right hand delivers me. The LORD will fulfill his purpose for me; thy steadfast love, O LORD, endures for ever. Do not forsake the work of thy hands.
138:7-8, RSV

The LORD is gracious and compassionate, slow to anger and rich in love. The Lord is good to all; he has compassion on all he has made.
145:8-9, NIV

GOD THE
PROMISE-KEEPER

God's promises are like the stars; the
darker the night, the brighter they
shine.
David Nicholas

The Lord's promise is sure. He speaks no careless word; all he says is purest truth, like silver seven times refined.
12:6, TLB

May the LORD answer you when you are in distress; may the name of the God of Jacob protect you. . . . May he give you the desire of your heart and make all your plans succeed.
20: 1, 4, NIV

The poor will eat and be satisfied; they who seek the LORD will praise him—may your hearts live forever!
22:26, NIV

The Lord is good and glad to teach the proper path to all who go astray; he will teach the ways that are right and best to those who humbly turn to him. And when we obey him, every path

he guides us on is fragrant with his
loving-kindness and his truth.
25:8-10, TLB

Many sorrows shall be to the wicked;
but he who trusts in the LORD, mercy
shall surround him.
32:10, NKJV

A righteous man may have many
troubles, but the LORD delivers him
from them all; he protects all his bones,
not one of them will be broken.
34:19-20, NIV

One thing God has spoken, two things
have I heard: that you, O God, are
strong, and that you, O LORD, are loving. Surely you will reward each per-
son according to what he has done.
62:11-12, NIV

Because he cleaves to me in love, I will deliver him; I will protect him, because he knows my name. When he calls to me, I will answer him; I will be with him in trouble, I will rescue him and honor him. With long life I will satisfy him, and show him my salvation.
91:14-16, RSV

This is my comfort in my affliction, for Your word has given me life.
119:50, NKJV

Your promises have been thoroughly tested, and your servant loves them.
119:140, NIV

WE LOVE YOUR
HOUSE, LORD

Every act of worship is its own justifi-
cation. It is rendering to God that of
which he is worthy.
Eric L. Mascall

But I through the abundance of thy steadfast love will enter thy house, I will worship toward thy holy temple in the fear of thee.
5:7, RSV

I love the house where you live, O LORD, the place where your glory dwells.
26:8, NIV

One thing have I asked of the LORD, that will I seek after; that I may dwell in the house of the LORD all the days of my life, to behold the beauty of the LORD, and to inquire in his temple.
27:4, RSV

Lord, here in your Temple we meditate upon your kindness and your love.
48:9, TLB

How lovely is your dwelling place, O LORD Almighty! My soul yearns, even faints for the courts of the LORD; my heart and my flesh cry out for the living God. Even the sparrow has found a home, and the swallow a nest for herself, where she may have her young—a place near your altar, O LORD Almighty, my King and my God. Blessed are those who dwell in your house; they are ever praising you.
84:1-4, NIV

Oh come, let us worship and bow down; let us kneel before the LORD our Maker. For He is our God, and we are the people of His pasture, and the sheep of His hand.
95:6-7, NKJV

I was glad when they said to me, "Let us go to the house of the Lord!"
122:1, RSV

SEEKING HIS FACE

To see his star is good, but to see his face is better.
D. L. Moody

In the morning, O LORD, you hear my voice; in the morning I lay my requests before you and wait in expectation.
5:3, NIV

My God, My God, why have You forsaken Me? Why are You so far from helping Me, and from the words of My groaning? O My God, I cry in the daytime, but You do not hear; and in the night season, and am not silent. . . . But You are He who took Me out of the womb; You made Me trust while I was on My mother's breasts. I was cast upon You from birth. From My mother's womb You have been My God. Be not far from Me, for trouble is near; for there is none to help.
22:1-2, 9-11, NKJV

There was a time when I wouldn't admit what a sinner I was. But my dishonesty made me miserable and filled my days with frustration. All day and all night your hand was heavy on me. My strength evaporated like water on a sunny day until I finally admitted all my sins to you and stopped trying to hide them. I said to myself, "I will confess them to the Lord." And you forgave me! All my guilt is gone.

32:3-5, *TLB*

I waited patiently for God to help me; then he listened and heard my cry. He lifted me out of the pit of despair, out from the bog and the mire, and set my feet on a hard, firm path and steadied me as I walked along. He has given me a new song to sing, of praises to our God. Now many will hear of the glorious things he did for me, and stand in awe be-

fore the Lord, and put their trust in
him.
40:1-3, TLB

As a hart longs for flowing streams, so
longs my soul for thee, O God. My
soul thirsts for God, for the living God.
When shall I come and behold the face
of God?
42:1-2, RSV

I long to dwell in your tent forever and
take refuge in the shelter of your wings.
For you have heard my vows, O God;
you have given me the heritage of
those who fear your name.
61:4-5, NIV

O God, You are my God; early will I
seek You; my soul thirsts for You; my
flesh longs for You in a dry and thirsty
land where there is no water.
63:1, NKJV

Answer me, O LORD, for thy steadfast love is good; according to thy abundant mercy, turn to me. Hide not thy face from thy servant; for I am in distress, make haste to answer me. Draw near to me, redeem me, set me free because of my enemies!
69:16-18, RSV

Hear my prayer, O LORD; let my cry come to thee! Do not hide thy face from me in the day of my distress! Incline thy ear to me; answer me speedily in the day when I call! For my days pass away like smoke, and my bones burn like a furnace. . . . But thou, O LORD, art enthroned for ever; thy name endures to all generations.
102:1-3, 12, RSV

When I called, you answered me; you made me bold and stouthearted.
138:3, NIV

A GODLY LIFE

God rules in the realms to which he is admitted.
Mary Welch

Mark this well: The Lord has set apart the redeemed for himself. Therefore he will listen to me and answer when I call to him. Stand before the Lord in awe, and do not sin against him. Lie quietly upon your bed in silent meditation. Put your trust in the Lord, and offer him pleasing sacrifices.
4:3-5, TLB

He whose walk is blameless and who does what is righteous, who speaks the truth from his heart and has no slander on his tongue . . . He who does these things will never be shaken.
15:2-3, 5, NIV

Remember not the sins of my youth and my rebellious ways; according to your love remember me, for you are good, O LORD.
25:7, NIV

Examine me, O LORD, and prove me; try my mind and my heart. For Your lovingkindness is before my eyes, and I have walked in Your truth.

26:2-3, NKJV

Blessed is the man who makes the LORD his trust, who does not look to the proud, to those who turn aside to false gods.

40:4, NIV

The greatest of men or the lowest—both alike are nothing in his sight. They weigh less than air on scales.

Don't become rich by extortion and robbery; if your riches increase, don't be proud. God has said it many times, that power belongs to him (and also, O Lord, steadfast love belongs to you). He rewards each one of us according to what our works deserve.

62:9-12, TLB

Praise the LORD. Blessed is the man who fears the LORD, who greatly delights in his commandments! His descendants will be mighty in the land; the generation of the upright will be blessed. Wealth and riches are in his house; and his righteousness endures for ever.
112:1-3, RSV

Unless the LORD builds the house, its builders labor in vain. Unless the LORD watches over the city, the watchmen stand guard in vain.
127:1, NIV

Search me, O God, and know my heart; try me, and know my anxieties; and see if there is any wicked way in me, and lead me in the way everlasting.
139:23-24, NKJV

GOD'S WORD

I did not go through the Book. The Book went through me.

A. W. Tozer

Blessed is the man who does not walk in the counsel of the wicked or stand in the way of sinners or sit in the seat of mockers. But his delight is in the law of the LORD, and on his law he meditates day and night.

1:1-2, NIV

Teach me your way, O LORD, and I will walk in your truth; give me an undivided heart, that I may fear your name.

86:11, NIV

So teach us to number our days that we may get a heart of wisdom.

90:12, RSV

But the mercy of the LORD is from everlasting to everlasting on those who fear Him, and His righteousness to children's children, To such as keep His covenant, and to those

who remember His commandments
to do them.
103:17-18, NKJV

How can men be wise? The only way
to begin is by reverence for God. For
growth in wisdom comes from obey-
ing his laws. Praise his name forever.
111:10, TLB

How can a young man keep his way
pure? By living according to your word.
I seek you with all my heart; do not let
me stray from your commands. I have
hidden your word in my heart that I
might not sin against you.
119:9-11, NIV

Your word is a lamp to my feet and a
light for my path.
119:105, NIV

GOD'S RIGHTEOUSNESS
AND JUDGMENT

God is indeed merciful and gracious,
but he is also righteous.
The Heidelberg Catechism

The LORD shall judge the peoples; judge me, O LORD, according to my righteousness, and according to my integrity within me. Oh, let the wickedness of the wicked come to an end, but establish the just; for the righteous God tests the hearts and minds. My defense is of God, who saves the upright in heart. God is a just judge, and God is angry with the wicked every day.

7:8-11, NKJV

The LORD is in his holy temple, the LORD's throne is in heaven; his eyes behold, his eyelids test, the children of men. The LORD tests the righteous and the wicked, and his soul hates him that loves violence. . . . For the LORD is righteous, he loves righteous deeds; the upright shall behold his face.

11:4-5, 7, RSV

Against you, you only, have I sinned
and done what is evil in your sight, so
that you are proved right when you
speak and justified when you judge.
Surely I was sinful at birth, sinful from
the time my mother conceived me.
Surely you desire truth in the inner
parts; you teach me wisdom in the
inmost place.
51:4-6, NIV

My lips will shout for joy when I sing
praise to you—I, whom you have redeemed. My tongue will tell of your
righteous acts all day long, for those
who wanted to harm me have been
put to shame and confusion.
71:23-24, NIV

How we thank you, Lord! Your
mighty miracles give proof that you
care.

"Yes," the Lord replies, "and when I am ready, I will punish the wicked! Though the earth shakes and all its people live in turmoil, yet its pillars are firm, for I have set them in place!"
75:1-3, TLB

Say among the nations, "The LORD reigns." The world is firmly established, it cannot be moved; he will judge the peoples with equity. Let the heavens rejoice, let the earth be glad; let the sea resound, and all that is in it; let the fields be jubilant, and everything in them. Then all the trees of the forest will sing for joy; they will sing before the LORD, for he comes, he comes to judge the earth. He will judge the world in righteousness and the peoples in his truth.
96:10-13, NIV

SALVATION AND ETERNAL LIFE

The salvation of a single soul is more important than the production or preservation of all the epics and tragedies in the world.
C. S. Lewis

But I have trusted in Your mercy; my heart shall rejoice in Your salvation. I will sing to the LORD, because He has dealt bountifully with me.

13:5-6, NKJV

The salvation of the righteous comes from the LORD; he is their stronghold in time of trouble. The LORD helps them and delivers them; he delivers them from the wicked and saves them, because they take refuge in him.

37:39-40, NIV

I have told everyone the good news that you forgive people's sins. I have not been timid about it, as you well know, O Lord. I have not kept this good news hidden in my heart, but have proclaimed your loving-kindness and truth to all the congregation.

40:9-10, TLB

Create in me a clean heart, O God, and renew a steadfast spirit within me. Do not cast me away from Your presence, and do not take Your Holy Spirit from me. Restore to me the joy of Your salvation, and uphold me by Your generous Spirit.
51:10-12, NKJV

May God be gracious to us and bless us and make his face shine upon us, that your ways may be known on earth, your salvation among all nations.
67:1-2, NIV

Nevertheless I am continually with thee; thou dost hold my right hand. Thou dost guide me with thy counsel, and afterward thou wilt receive me to glory. Whom have I in heaven but thee? And there is nothing upon earth that I desire besides thee. My flesh and

my heart may fail, but God is the strength of my heart and my portion for ever. For lo, those who are far from thee shall perish; thou dost put an end to those who are false to thee. But for me it is good to be near God; I have made the Lord GOD my refuge, that I may tell of all thy works.
73:23-28, RSV

Sing to the LORD a new song, for he has done marvelous things; his right hand and his holy arm have worked salvation for him. The LORD has made his salvation known and revealed his righteousness to the nations. He has remembered his love and his faithfulness to the house of Israel; all the ends of the earth have seen the salvation of our God.
98:1-3, NIV

O Israel, hope in the Lord; for he is loving and kind and comes to us with armloads of salvation.
130:7, TLB

PRAISE HIM!

When I think of God, my heart is so full of joy that the notes leap and dance as they leave my pen.

Franz Joseph Haydn

The LORD lives! Praise be to my Rock!
Exalted be God my Savior!
18:46, NIV

Lift up your heads, O gates! and be
lifted up, O ancient doors! that the
King of glory may come in. Who is the
king of glory? The LORD, strong and
mighty, the LORD, mighty in battle! Lift
up your heads, O gates! and be lifted
up, O ancient doors! that the King of
glory may come in. Who is this King
of glory? The LORD of hosts, he is the
King of glory!
24:7-10, RSV

Praise the Lord, you angels of his;
praise his glory and his strength. Praise
him for his majestic glory, the glory of
his name. Come before him clothed in
sacred garments.
29:1-2, TLB

Thou hast turned for me my mourning into dancing; thou hast loosed my sackcloth and girded me with gladness, that my soul may praise thee and not be silent. O LORD my God, I will give thanks to thee for ever.
30:11-12, RSV

I will bless the LORD at all times; His praise shall continually be in my mouth. My soul shall make its boast in the LORD; the humble shall hear of it and be glad. Oh, magnify the LORD with me, and let us exalt His name together.
34:1-3, NKJV

Clap your hands, all you nations; shout to God with cries of joy. How awesome is the LORD Most High, the great King over all the earth! . . . God has ascended amid shouts of joy, the LORD amid the sounding of trumpets. Sing

praises to God, sing praises; sing praises to our King, sing praises.
47:1-2, 5-6, NIV

Sing aloud to God our strength; make a joyful shout to the God of Jacob. Raise a song and strike the timbrel, the pleasant harp with the lute.
81:1-2, NKJV

It is good to praise the LORD and make music to your name, O Most High, to proclaim your love in the morning and your faithfulness at night, to the music of the ten-stringed lyre and the melody of the harp. For you make me glad by your deeds, O LORD; I sing for joy at the works of your hands. How great are your works, O LORD, How profound your thoughts! The senseless man does not know, fools do not understand, that though the wicked spring up like grass and all evildoers

flourish, they will be forever destroyed.
But you, O LORD, are exalted forever.
92:1-8, NIV

Oh, give thanks to the Lord, for he is
good; his loving-kindness continues
forever.

Give thanks to the God of gods, for
his loving-kindness continues forever.
Give thanks to the Lord of lords, for
his loving-kindness continues forever.
Praise him who alone does mighty miracles, for his loving-kindness continues forever. Praise him who made the
heavens, for his loving-kindness continues forever. Praise him who planted
the water within the earth, for his
loving-kindness continues forever.
Praise him who made the heavenly
lights, for his loving-kindness continues forever: the sun to rule the day, for
his loving-kindness continues forever;

and the moon and stars at night, for his loving-kindness continues forever.
136:1-9, TLB

Praise the LORD from the earth, you great sea creatures and all ocean depths, lightning and hail, snow and clouds, stormy winds that do his bidding, you mountains and all hills, fruit trees and all cedars, wild animals and all cattle, small creatures and flying birds, kings of the earth and all nations, you princes and all rulers on earth, young men and maidens, old men and children. . . . Praise the Lord.
148:7-12, 14, NIV